SONGBOOK

SONGBOOK

the lyrics and music of

STEVEN HEIGHTON

Published by ECW Press
665 Gerrard Street East
Toronto, Ontario, Canada M4M 1Y2
416-694-3348 / info@ecwpress.com

 Editor for the Press: Michael Holmes /
a misFit Book
Copyeditor: Jen Albert
MISFIT Cover design: Jessica Albert
Author photo: Ginger Pharand

LIBRARY AND ARCHIVES CANADA CATALOGUING
IN PUBLICATION

Title: Songbook : the lyrics and music of Steven Heighton / Steven Heighton ; introduction by Ginger Pharand

Names: Heighton, Steven, 1961-2022, author. | Pharand, Ginger, author of introduction, etc.

Description: Song lyrics, with chord symbols.

Identifiers: Canadiana (print) 2023058988X | Canadiana (ebook) 20230590071

ISBN 978-1-77041-771-7 (softcover)
ISBN 978-1-77852-300-7 (ePub)
ISBN 978-1-77852-301-4 (PDF)

Subjects: LCSH: Songs, English—Texts.

Classification: LCC ML54 .6 .H465 2024 | DDC 782.42164/0268—dc23

This book is funded in part by the Government of Canada. *Ce livre est financé en partie par le gouvernement du Canada.* We acknowledge the support of the Canada Council for the Arts. *Nous remercions le Conseil des arts du Canada de son soutien.* We acknowledge the funding support of the Ontario Arts Council (OAC), an agency of the Government of Ontario. We also acknowledge the support of the Government of Ontario through the Ontario Book Publishing Tax Credit, and through Ontario Creates.

PRINTED AND BOUND IN CANADA   PRINTING: MARQUIS   5   4   3   2   1

CONTENTS

Long Road Home to the Forbidden Technique, or Finding Freedom in Constraint

This book is a new relation to the 2011 ECW title *Workbook: Memos & Dispatches on Writing*. In *Workbook*, Steve shared thoughts on the creative life, writing as a profession, and advice he wished he could give to his younger self. A decade later, as part of his writer-in-residence position at Athabasca University, he published the text of a keynote speech, "The Virtues of Disillusionment," which tracked, among other ideas, the distance in years between when he first perceived the advice for his younger self and when he finally began to live by it. He had begun, *finally* he said, to embrace the great lyric from Mahalia Jackson to "live the life I sing about in my songs." It was more than a metaphor. For Steve, it meant committing himself to writing music after years of channelling that impulse into his poetry and prose. This songbook should not be viewed as a departure from his literary legacy into a final artistic desire line, but a convergence, an invitation to formally meet the music that was in him and his work all along.

Steve was a creative polyglot from the start. Not only a precociously skilled visual artist, one especially gifted at caricatures and quick ink sketches, he also completed his first novel at age ten on a plastic typewriter his parents had given him. His father, John, recalls that Steve emerged from his bedroom one evening and requested a ride to the Toronto offices of McClelland & Stewart, where, Steve explained, he'd sent his manuscript and they wanted to speak with him about it. His father obliged, and Steve sat in one of the press's offices with an editor and listened to the critique with the same seriousness about his work he retained all his life. He politely thanked everyone for their time and returned home to his desk and the edits! Despite this promising and focused early commitment to writing, it was in music that he found creative passion. A quiet, bookish child most comfortable in his room drawing and reading and studying the globe, Steve's introduction to language as a lyric art came through his father's dramatic recitations of poetry and, even more impressively to Steve, a vast repertoire of songs.

> My father was a human jukebox. Cue him with a request while he was driving and he'd quote verse by anyone from Robert Service to Emily Dickinson, or sing songs by anyone from Paul Robeson to Cream. He made the forms seem interchangeable. And when he quoted poems like "The Ballad of Sir Patrick Spens" or "The Highwayman," he recited so rhythmically and melodically they might as well have been sung.

If that description is familiar, maybe you once encountered Steve himself when he was holding a guitar. A serious listener as well as a musician, he could play back almost any song pitched to him. On the rare occasions he didn't already know the song, he would study a singer or fellow player (or ask to hold a cell phone up to his ear in a kind of aural download) for only moments before rendering a passable if not fully impressive version of his own.

In high school, he took up the electric guitar and formed a band called Acröpölis. (Steve: "Named after myself—Acropolis, High Town, with an umlaut over not one but *both* of the *o*'s—now that tells you everything you need to know about us as a band.") The brief career of Acröpölis notwithstanding, Steve's early notebooks are filled with a fairly equal balance between political and romantic songs, the lyrics in urgent, minuscule print, a detail he found telling—and moving—when he revisited them. He declared it was proof that even he hadn't trusted his music to take up space in the world. Beyond his tentative lyrics, he could also be a brutal critic of his own playing, particularly his strumming, which he attributed to wanting "to create the impression of a big, compelling band, when it was really just me, my guitar, and my harmonica—i.e., like a scared animal puffing itself up to look larger in the face of a threat."

Guitar lessons ad in the Queen's Journal,
January 1983

In 1981, he set out hitchhiking around Australia with a big red Suzuki guitar he bought for $100 Australian upon landing. He taped a busking list to the top of the guitar, where it remains to this day, though now its role is more the first faded shred of his considerable musical archive, the yellow paper barely visible among the other song lists that accumulated there over the years. At Queen's University in the early 1980s, he began to sing and perform with Mary Huggard and Lynne "Wayward" Wilson on campus and around Kingston. Graduation, travel, and marriage followed. By the time he and Mary settled in Kingston, he was committed to a career in writing and had given up music to assume "my life sentence as a poet." He would return to writing songs briefly in 1990, then not seriously again until the mid-2010s. Despite his dedication to the written word (and making a living at it), he refused to fully abandon the silent pact he made with himself to hold music at the centre of his creative life.

When I first started writing poetry my strong impulse was to rhyme, not because I didn't know what free verse was or the reasons it had evolved, not because I equated poetry with doggerel and Valentine's Day verse, but because I'd already spent several years (between the ages

9

of sixteen and twenty) writing songs, hundreds of them. Also, because for me poetry was simply song by other means. Reading poets like Dylan Thomas had convinced me that it was possible to sing in one's poems, that words could bear musical valence, that absent a guitar and drum kit they could accompany themselves, enact melodies and carve out cadences that would atone for the abstraction of mere words—glyphs—on the page. The written word is a modest medium. A word on the page is nothing but a symbol, mere code, whereas sung words are actual wave forms that, depending on the shape of the waves, can caress or batter the body of a listener. My instinct was to try to do that via poetry, like the poets I loved. . . . I soon learned that poetry with musical valence, especially if it involved rhyme, was dimly viewed.

Anyone who saw him at a reading might have caught sight of his boot tapping out the metre, his shoulders shrugging the rhythm, the cords of his neck flexing, his whole body moving in the recognizable sway of a cleric shuckling in prayer—or, a musician keeping time. For thirty years, he would channel the songs in him into poems, short stories, novels, and essays.

In 2010, having taken up hockey as a forty-nine-year-old, Steve sustained a potentially life-threatening injury to his throat on the ice. When the doctor gave him the order not to talk, he also included that Steve likely wouldn't ever sing again. "*Do* you sing?" the doctor asked. The question unnerved Steve, shook buried dreams awake, though his creative response to the epiphany would take several years more to fully surface. *Epiphany*, from the Greek, of course, a manifestation, breaking through, surfacing. When the songs began this time, Steve was a different artist and man. He raised his daughter, Elena, and built a career as a writer. He had lived long enough and worked hard enough that he knew how to seize an inspiration, contain the early energy within a draft, and then interrogate it ruthlessly until it yielded its gold.

He extended confidence and skill to songwriting so that his curiosity about this new material remained greater than the anxiety of surrendering to beginner status again in his fifties ("it gives you grey hairs but keeps you young"). The resumption of songwriting also allowed him to utilize rhyme, that mockable offence in the modern literary world. Forced to abandon it in his twenties, despite it appealing to his earliest inspirations, he relished the opportunity to return. His song notes are filled with columns of line-end rhymes, slant rhymes, internal rhymes, silly, bawdy, cliché rhymes. He was giddy, drunk with the possibilities. He felt the constraint forced his mind to reach further to discover where a song would end up because of the rhymes that revealed it. "How good to come back to it now," he wrote. He completed fourteen songs between 2015 and 2020, in addition to publishing six books.

After a half decade of accumulating new music, in 2019 the fates placed Steve on a ferry with Chris Brown of Wolfe Island Records. He approached Hugh Christopher, fully expecting Chris to appreciate the songs but not the singer. He only wanted to make some demos to pass on to professional musicians for them to record. Chris was receptive and immediately invited Steve to drop by and play for him. The invitation spooked Steve, and a few more ferry rides elapsed before they would speak again despite often sharing the same boat— on one occasion Steve even hid, worried: "He'll think I'm stalking him." Eventually, nerves settled and the two met at the Post Office, Wolfe Island Records' studio. Not only did Chris recognize the songs as strong, but he encouraged Steve to sing them. Steve took it as a kind of blessing from one of his earliest and most beloved songfathers: the same scenario occurred at the beginning of Kris Kristofferson's career when he went to Nashville looking for "a real singer" to sing his songs. Chris Brown said, when Steve quoted this line, "What if you *are* the real singer for your songs?"

The Devil's Share was recorded in 2019 and 2020, its final sessions overlapping the beginning of the pandemic, further complicating the project and challenging Steve's resolve in various practical ways. He felt urgency, however, a need to finally take his own advice. He was then working on *The Virtues of Disillusionment* and all too aware how inertia can swallow one's quiet aspirations and years. The album was completed and released in 2021. Largely comprised of new material, it also contained two songs started in 1990. Of those two, only "Don't Remember Me" appears as he finished it in 1991. The second, "Always Almost Leaving," was unfinished until 2019, when, struggling to complete it in a late night songwriting session at my kitchen table on Wolfe Island, he started throwing out descriptive phrases. We went back and forth. "Safe in harbour, oceans . . ." "Seas, changes" "Sea change . . . Key change!" The final verse to a thirty-year-old song was then written in half an hour.

As with his poetry, dreams were a frequent source of lyrics and music, the insistence of what Steve called "the nightmind" into his writing life. Four of the songs on the album came directly from dreams, including "The Devil's Share," the first verse and chorus of which he described as hearing playing in a tinny old radio sitting in the open window of a country house. With "Six Months at the Worst," he woke with just a few lines but the riff that anchors the song. Unable to read or write music, he drew the melody progression as waves and arrows on a scrap of paper. Inspired by Kris Kristofferson's description of how he wrote "Why Me?" and awakened from a dream by fireworks on Wolfe Island, "New Year's Song" appeared in the early hours of New Year's 2020. Steve called it a gospel song, one that, like all spiritual anthems, signals an abrupt release from the lie of separateness. Rattled, exposed, and energized by overlapping experiences in that hypnogogic state, he wrote the first verse and bridge in a single go and they remain largely unedited from the initial draft. He said if there was a theme to *The Devil's Share*, it was in the first and last songs, between body and soul: beginning with an unrepentant celebration of sex as a metaphor for embodiment

Wayward (Mary Huggard, Lynne Wilson, Steven Heighton)
playing at the Quiet Pub on the Queen's campus, 1984

in a disembodied age and ending with a man cracked open, finally and gratefully, in complete surrender to life, love, and song.

Steve would often start a song with a riff, a melodic progression, and he said if he played it often enough, it would begin to suggest the words to fit it. In the case of the fourth dream song, "Sometimes Even Liars Tell the Truth," he had been working for weeks with a riff, but no lyrics had come until I recounted a dream of my own that included the title line. He was listening and noodling around on the guitar and stopped. "Say it again." After singing the line several times against the riff, he had the "in" and we quickly built the song around it. The remaining songs on *The Devil's Share* paid tribute to various songfathers or their musical forms (Cohen, Kristofferson), but even as he completed the album, Steve was already writing new material, sometimes three or four songs in various draft forms at once. The songs for the second album represented a new musical confidence, some of which resulted from playing music publicly and preparing to do that more often. Performance is a wild card, the antithesis of the controlled editorial space where long-overlooked howlers in a text are furtively deleted at the last moment on final proofs.

Instead, performance is full exposure, maximum vulnerability. If the monitor or the mic levels are off or a COVID plastic screen deadens the acoustics or a loud audience member claps off-time, those "wave forms" of sound can bury lyrics that were so carefully constructed on the page or managed in the studio. The variables at work onstage, the real-time calculus of performance, terrified and thrilled Steve. If you blow it, he said, it might be the only version of the song the audience ever hears. But there was also the rare joy of the ever-present now, just as he felt whenever he got to be on the ice in hockey, that thrill of the do-over every time you played the song. For a writer who had lived bound to the exacting, captious, editorial eye and ear, and took those same standards into the studio, he said performing was a moment in the hands of the gods to some degree, every time. There was no "nailing it to the page" onstage.

The songs that followed *The Devil's Share* and included here were never publicly played set to their music with the exception of "Read the Sign" and "The Butcher's Bill," which we played in Fernie, B.C., in December 2021, at Steve's final gig. With *Songbook*, their interpretations will belong to every musician who plays them. That is fitting given Steve's lifelong appreciation for and devotion to "approximations" in poetry. He loved to flip genres, challenge the structure, and does it several times in the newer songs, such as setting Melville's "The Portent" to a driving Americana acoustic beat, or indicating in the notes for "Want It All on Credit" that he imagined both mournful Russian guitar and a rapper in the song's bridge. ("My dream date in this case would be Immortal Technique," he wrote.) He frequently explored how tempo or voicing could alter a lyric or change a song's effect entirely. In November of 2021, he discovered the melody line in Gloria Gaynor's disco classic, "I Will Survive," and played it daily for weeks on his Taylor acoustic (and we performed it at the Fernie show, with him whaling happily on the guitar while I sang). He wanted to spotlight the melody buried in the mix, foregrounding what people had always heard in the song without realizing it. In that same way, the new songs are an inspirational and genre shuffle, reflecting the breadth of Steve's influences, including tributes to John Prine ("The Buddha of Song") and Leon Redbone ("Still Ain't Misbehavin'"), while staying true to his thematic legacy: meditations on love, sex, death, religion, the vanity and folly of egoic stubbornness, and, of course, his political conscience, evident in songs like "The Butcher's Bill," a searing indictment of the global war machine stealing the youth of a nation through propaganda and conscription. With the exception of "Looking Back," written in the mid-1980s, all the unrecorded songs were composed between 2019 and 2022. The final song Steve worked on was "Last Living Woman Alive," which he completed in February of 2022, though still complaining in March that he was "coveting a better bossa nova" to be written into the middle of it.

Singing with Ray Robertson at the Royal Tavern,
Kingston, February 13, 2020

Those who knew Steve only through his poetry and literary work may find *Songbook* unfamiliar terrain in places. In his music, however, the formal writer surrendered to an unguarded, passionate, often playful, and wholly embodied form of artmaking. Those who knew him personally will recognize it immediately; his convictions, humour, and generous heart are clearly on display. When asked in 2021 why he chose to immerse himself in making music right at the moment he did, Steve answered in what now reads as a hauntingly prescient response: "I decided it was now or never; and it was."

The title of this introduction came from Steve, his own description of the long-delayed reconnection with writing music. In these pages, I have tried to provide a brief glimpse into the songwriting soul of him so that anyone encountering his music and his lyrics will share in that connection. The final lines, which say everything else he wanted known, I leave to Steve as well.

> Some people believe that youth is the time of maximum sincerity and passion and that we all get more ironic and sardonic with age. It seems my life arc is aimed in the opposite direction. As another hero of mine (John Prine) said, "The heart gets bored with the mind and it changes you." These songs signify and celebrate that change.

GINGER PHARAND

KINGSTON, ONTARIO, 2023

16

THE
DEVIL'S
SHARE

The Devil's Share

[Capo 3–5, so played chords differ]

Em   Am   B7   C7add7 B7 Em :||

[Verses 1 & 2]
Em
We're making so much romance

      Am
We've got extra here to spare

   B7
So it hardly makes a difference

    C7add7 B7   Em
If the devil takes his share

We're making so much love now
We put extra in the bank
And though heaven takes the credit
It's the devil you should thank

[Chorus]
Am
We're sharing so much sugar

        C
The bees are getting jealous

B7
Businesses are going broke

    C7add7   B7   Em
There's nothing they can sell us

[Verses 3, 4 & 5, same pattern as 1 & 2]
We're planning to protract this
With some help from down below
The Feds'll try to tax this
But it's the devil that we owe

We make each moment midnight
And hope the sun don't notice
Though our neighbours seem annoyed now
Here's a note that they just wrote us
Weeks or more we're walled in
And we never go outdoors
And our creditors are calling
And the bailiff's at the door

[Chorus]

Am
We're sharing so much sugar

          C
The honeybees are jealous

B7
CNN has gone off-air

          C7add7   B7   Em
There's nothing it can tell us

[Instrumental]
Am   Em   E5add#11 [022300] C7 Bmaj11 B11 Baug Em
:|| B

[Verses 7, 8 & 9, same pattern as verse 1]
Sometimes it's sweet to occupy
These bodies we sublet

22

God thinks He's the landlord
But the devil owns the debt

They say for any joy you steal
A bill is on the way
But if lawyers send the invoice
It's the devil you should pay

Now Dante and the devil both
Provide for lovers well
They cancel fees and cut the keys
To the cooler rooms in hell

[Chorus]

Am
We're sharing so much sugar

            C
The bees are in the breadline

   B7
The taxman's taken up the sax

     C7add7   B7   Em
And Death is missing deadlines

[Instrumental, just one iteration this time]

[Final verses, same pattern]
What started as a spark here
Now feels a lot like flame
If my kisses leave a mark here
It's the devil you should blame

We're making so much romance
We've got extra here to spare
So it hardly makes a difference
If the devil takes his share

Let the devil take his share
Let the devil take his share

When You Finally Learn to Love

[Capo 5]

[Verse 1]
C
I was losing my shirt

Aboard the con man's yacht
    Em7
At a table of baize by the pool.
       Am
He said, "Losing is worst, but winning gets lonely
        F
When you run out of friends you can fool."
Dm   E
Then he confided this guidance to me
      Am   F
And it stunned me to hear him say it—
C   **[run down to Am]**   Am/G
"Son, when you finally learn to love
      F   E   Am---------E--------
Don't let it be too late."

[Verse 2]
Am
I caught Don Juan

With his jeans still on

        Dm   Am
In a bar watching country TV.

"I'm too tired to check out the women," he sighed,
                    F   E
"And now they've quit looking back at me."
Dm   E
Then he nodded at words up on the screen,
        Am   F
I guess he preferred not to say it—

C   [run down to Am]   Am/G
Lord, when I finally learn to love

        F   E   Am
Don't let it be too late.

[Chorus]

F   C
When I finally learn to love

        E   Am
Don't let it be too late.
        F   [run down to Dm]   Dm/C
Let it not be said when I'm stone-cold dead
                G   G7
He knew the word but he wouldn't say it.
        F   C
So if you know the tune lay it down soon
        E   Am
If you're feeling a prayer then pray it.

```
F              C
```
Lord when you finally learn to love

```
        Dm        Am   [run back up to C]
```
Don't let it be too late.

[Verse 3]
Another old fraud
Was getting nearer to God
Downing gin and recounting his crash.
He said, "Do you reckon there's girls after greed
Or does love disappear with the cash?"
And then he scribbled this note on the bill
After hinting he hoped that I'd pay it—
Friend, when you finally learn to love
Don't let it be too late.

[Verse 4]
A woman who knew me
Once promised to show me
And she taught me all night until waking.
"You tell me you don't know what love is," she said,
"But you know this is love that we're making."
And now every time her gift crosses my mind
I wish I could finally repay it.
If I ever do learn to say the word
Don't let it be too late.

[Chorus—but resolve on A, not Am, then go to Am to start bridge]

[Bridge]
```
Am                     C
```
The head believes it's the one in charge

27

```
       F            E
```
And the heart's a lowly driver

```
    C                         F      C
```
But when the crash comes, and come it will,

```
E              E7      Am     [run up to C]
```
There'll be just one survivor.

[Verse 5]
On a bench in the park
As day leaned into dark
He was sitting in his famous grey suit.
He'd been dead for a year but looked no worse for wear
And I said, "Leonard, what got you through it?"
He just hummed a few bars of a song,
Said, "If you work out the words you can play it.
And friend, when you finally learn to love
Don't let it be too late."

[Chorus, then repeat last line two extra times]

When You Finally Learn to Love Reprise

"Meant to be a fun, rocking, ridiculous parody of my own song (which means there's way more than a little truth in it)."

Open G

[Intro]
C   C7   F   D7   G   G7   C

[Verse 1]
If I ever wrote a country song
       F   C
It might go a little bit like this
          [run down to A]
I'd want to seem like a cross between
    D7   G
Late Cash and early Kris
   C   C7
But they'd sing a tune about dyin' or doin'
   F   C
And I'd be a liar to play it

Lord, when I finally learn to love
     G   G7   C
Don't let it be too late

[Chorus]

G
Lord, when I finally learn to love

      C   G
Don't let it be too late.

G
Let it not be said when I'm stone-cold dead

          A   D
He knew the word but he would not say it

   G
So if you know the tune, lay it down soon

[Vary with each chorus]

               C   G
[1] There's no time to dither and wait]
[2] There's no time to ruminate/cogitate]
[3] If you're feeling a prayer then pray it]
Lord, when I finally learn to love

        D   G
Don't let it be too late.

[Verse 2]
I thought I'd got life figured out
When I was still back in school
I thought I could tell what love was, well
I was just an educated fool
Now I'm older but not a lot bolder
It makes me ashamed to say it
Lord when I finally learn to love
Don't let it be too late

[Chorus]

[Bridge]

      C

Got a marriage and a mortgage and a daughter and son

        G

And the doctor'd say when every check-up was done

        A   D

"You're as right as rain," so why do I feel this pain in my heart?

[Verse 3]
If I ever wrote a country song
It might be something along these lines
I'd want it to feel like a combo deal
Half Hank and half John Prine
But they'd sing a tune about a love they're pursuing
And I'm known to hesitate
Lord, when I finally learn to love
Don't let it be too late

Working on The Devil's Share,
Wolfe Island

31

Don't Remember Me

[Capo 3 or 5]

G   Em   :|| G

[Verse 1]

     C   G   D   Em
No, I don't remember how we met

 C   G   D   Em
When or where or what was said

     C   G   D   Em
And I don't remember how I fell

     C   D   G
And I don't remember you

[Verse 2, same pattern]
And I don't recall the time or place
We first lay down and made our peace
And I won't remember how your face
Opened like a sea

[Chorus]

     C   D   Em
And I don't remember you

   C   D   G
No, I don't remember you

   C   D   Em
No, I don't remember you

```
       C     D      G
```
And you don't remember me

[Verse 3]
All the ways we loved have slipped my mind
Like the letters I forget to send
Souvenirs of grass and sand
Carried home from the sea

[Chorus]
And I don't remember you
No, I don't remember you
And I don't remember you
And you don't remember me

[Verse 4]
And I don't remember why you left
When or where or what was said
And the things you felt I've had to guess
All these years that I've been free

[Chorus]
And I don't remember you
No, I don't remember you
And I don't remember you
Do you still remember me?

Sometimes Even Liars Tell the Truth

Lyrics by Steven Heighton and Ginger Pharand
Music by Steven Heighton

[Capo 2 or 3]

[Intro: Em for 2 measures, then:]
E5add#11 [022300]　　C7　　　　B7　　　C7 B11 Em　C7 B11:||

[Verse 1]

E5add#11　　　　　C7
When a man of his kind says the words "I love you"

B7　　　　　　　　Em　　C7 B11
You might tell yourself that's nothing new

E5add#11　　　　　　　　　C7
And when he promises that there's no one else above you

B7　　　　　　　　　　Em
You might want to ask him for some proof

C/G
And when he makes his vows

Am
And he tells you how

Em　　　　E5add#11　B7　　　C7 B11
He and only he alone will do—

E5add#11　　　　　　C7
When a man of his sort says he'll always love you

　　B7　　　　　　　　　Em　　　C7 B11
Well, sometimes even liars tell the truth

34

[Verse 2]
What does it mean to mean it when you're a man like he is
What does it take to start out new?
If there's a way to change men, girl you've never seen it
And there's no telling what they'll change into

C/G
And when he gets to pledging

Am
And you fear he's hedging

Em   E5add#11   B7   C7 B11
And not saying what he really feels for you

E5add#11   C7
When a man of his sort swears he'll always love you

[hold C7 this time] B7   Em   C7 B11
Well, sometimes even liars tell the truth

[Verse 3]
Trying to trust the right words, trying to track the lies
Is work enough for any heart to do
So many times in love, conditions will apply
Can you trust they don't apply to you?

C/G
And when he swears he'll show you

Am
And he claims to know you

Em   E5add#11   B7   C7 B11
You can't help fearing it's all flowing too smooth—

E5add#11   C7
But when a man of his sort says he'll always love you

[hold C7 again]   B7   Em

Well, sometimes even liars tell the truth

     C7   B7

Well, sometimes even liars tell

C7   B7

Sometimes even liars

C7   B7   Em

Sometimes even liars tell the truth

2020 (Cohen's Future)

[Capo 5, so actual chords Am, Em11 [020203]/A, F, C, Dm, E7, etc.]

Em   Bm11/A [x04430] :||

Em   C   G   Am
We're in the future, mister, and it's just as he forecast it

  Em   C   G   Am
It's each one for their ego and our ethics are elastic

    Em   C   G   Am
We're living in the next phase, and it's just as he projected

    Em   C   G   Am   Em   Bm11/A :||
The prophets' voices fade out and their killers get elected

    Em   C   G   Am
The new regime condemns you all, the rapists and the rapees

      Em   C   G   Am
As you pour across our border wall pretending you're escapees

  Em   C   G   B7
The new regime supplies live-stream of its latest retributions

  Em   C   G   B7
See drone's-eye bombings, sniper kills, see curbside executions

  Em   C   G   B7
Assassinations, threats, and coups, and ultimate solutions

      Em   C   G   Am   Em   Bm11/A :||
For refugees, for enemies, for Cubans, Arabs, Roossians

```
      Em            C            G            Am
We've entered the new epoch and it's much as he foretold us

      Em            C                    G            Am
It's Netflix while our neighbour screams and the next one over trolls us

      Em            C                G         B7
No Christ to spoil the stoning when you're online being hateful

      Em        C            G            B7
And if you find a good stone, I'm sure you mean to aim well

      Em            C            G            Am
And if a small voice whispers, "Maybe you yourself aren't blame-free

      Em        C            G                Am            C
You'd better holler louder or we'll nail you to the same tree"
```

[Bridge]

```
                    Em        G    A
I know some say it's mindless

                    C        Bm11/A   C
To speak of simple kindness

                    Em        G   Gb
But the Future is our present

                            B            Em   Bm11/A :||
And nothing less than love can bind us
```

```
Em                    C            G            Am
High time we took our countries back—back to the Middle Ages

      Em            C                G            Am
When we caged whatever crossed our lines and threw away the cages

      Em            C            G            B7
When we pried the babies from the breast, enslaved them or we sold them
```

```
Em              C              G              Am      Em  Bm11/A
```
We're in the Future and its fads are just as he foretold them

```
Em              C              G                    Am
```
Lies this size stop registering on old-school lie detectors

```
    Em          C              G              Am
```
We've mined your data anyhow and we've paid off the collectors

```
    Em          C              G          B7
```
This is the Future, sister, and it's just like his predictions

```
    Em              C                  G        Am      C
```
It's porn flicks while in quarantine, it's online crucifixions

[Bridge 2, same pattern as bridge 1]
I know some say it's spineless
To speak with simple kindness
But the Future is this present
And we can't let them define us

```
Em                  C              G          Am
```
A poor man will work for peanuts—that's advice a guy once gave me

```
Em          C                  G          Am
```
He said it like a priest might, like he figured it might save me

```
    Em          C              G              B7
```
Well, mister, you can take your scams and shove them up your assets

```
    Em              C                  G          B7
```
We're sick of how your Futures kill in all their modes and facets

```
    Em          C          G      Am
```
We're in the Future, mister, and it's just as he forecast it

```
    Em              C          G              B7
```
It's each one for their ego, and our prospects all look drastic

39

```
Em              C              G         Am
```
We're living in the next phase and it's just as he expected

```
    Em          C              G         Am
```
The singers' voices die out and the goons get re-elected

[Spoken afterward]
We're in the future, madam, and it's just as he foretold us
It's like we're Eve and Adam, living in a swampland someone's sold us

Six Months at the Worst

[Capo 2 or 3, so played chords differ]

[Intro]
G   C   Am   D :|| G

[Verse 1]
                  C/G   Am   D
They'll give you six months at the worst
G   C/G   Am   D
You'll have to say you're sorry first
G   Cmaj7/G   Am   D
"Sorry" isn't hard, you just say everything in reverse
G   C   Am   D   G
Your friends know lines you can rehearse

[Verse 2, same pattern]
It's nice to not get sent to jail
It's sweet when Papa pays the bail
Bright futures like your future need not be derailed
His lawyers handle the details

[Bridge]
Am
She's just a drunk girl

   G   D
With no choice to refuse you

Am
A drunk and drugged girl

G . D   A F C Eb Bb D
With no voice to accuse you

[Verse 3]
They say she's just a drunken girl
Passed out in her party dress and pearls
Some boys believe a drunk girl gets what she deserves
And cries for help all go unheard

[Verse 4]
She's Black, she's white, she's Brown, she's Native
They'll talk about the paths she strayed off
They'll make a list of all the drugs she should have stayed off
They'll ask what girls these days are made of

[Bridge 2, same pattern as bridge 1]
She's just a drunk girl
No reason to suspect you
A drunk and drugged girl
With no means to reject you

As you know ...

[Verse 5]
Behind a dumpster you leave her crying
For all you know she could be dying
If you get caught, why you just testify she's lying
It won't be you the system's trying

[Bridge 3]
You're just a drunk boy
No cop here to be your conscience
When people talk about tenderness

You suspect they know it's nonsense

Yeah you do . . .

[Intro riff repeats to fade]

Mixing The Devil's Share *with Chris Brown, February 2021*

One Breath

[Capo 2 (so played chords differ), G played with D on B string: 320033]

[Intro spoken over chords and arco bass]
```
Em              G
```
I'm just an ordinary traveller

```
Am                    Em
```
In this world I'm weary and perplexed

```
B7                  C       [run down to A]
```
I know fear's the great unraveller
```
                        B7
```
I know how many it infects

```
G           D           F       Em
```
But just when it seems that even *love* is just another word

```
C           D       Em
```
A word no better than the next

```
C           D       Em
```
There's one truth I always recollect

[Verse 1]
```
Em                      G
```
There's a certain late night languor

```
Am              Em  [run up to G]
```
That your kiss alone corrects

```
G       D   F   Em
```
And so this love grows ever stronger

```
    C       D   Em
```
From one breath to the next

[Verse 2]
Though strangers close their faces
And the oldest friend defects
I can sense you in the spaces
From one breath to the next

[Verse 3, different pattern after line 2]
Em   G
There's a kind of code between us

Am   Em
That each kiss and touch encrypts

B7   C   [run down to A]
A circuit that contains us

                      B7
And nothing disconnects

G   D F   Em
And this link is what sustains us

        C   D   Em
From one breath to the next

[Verse 4, same as 1 & 2]
The bitters we drink daily
They leave us shattered and unsexed
But your touch will still remake me
From one breath to the next

[Verse 5, same as 3]
They say we're all born liars—
I feel I really must object
Like the fool a mad king requires
You sing truths no one expects

And with your versions I will conspire
From one breath to the next

[Verse 6, same as 1 & 2]
I've noted your indifference
To empty words the world respects
It lives to talk, but love is just this listening
From one breath to the next

[Verse 7, different pattern after line 4]
Em   G
While colonels arm the children

Am   Em
While their researchers vivisect

B7   C   [run down to A]
And we get bilked and battered

                    B7
By the usual suspects

F   Em
And the haters find new ways to hate

        C   D   E
And shatter and reject

G   D   F   Em
We'll lie down and lodge our silent protest

        C   D   Em
From one breath to the next

[Verse 8, same as 1 & 2]
So stay beside this sleeper
The one your vigilance protects

Even now his love is travelling deeper
From one breath to the next

[Repeat refrain twice more, resolving on E major]

Forty years of song lists on Steve's red guitar

Another Kind of Worse

[Capo 5, so chords actually E7/Am/F, etc.]

[Intro]
B7   Em   B7   Em

[Verse 1]
    B7
Slip a slingblade in your pocket

      Em
Pack a pistol in your purse

        B7
Bomb those Persians in their mosque or

       Em
Shoot the shooter in our church

     C
But when it comes to the inner fight

       Em
We're all curiously averse

     B7
'Cause, brother, we ain't better

        C   B7   Em
We're just another kind of worse

[Verse 2]
Some say we'll hear angel choirs
If we just outshout the haters
Out-hate far-right online liars
And the fires all will fade out

But the only music we hear now
Are these sirens on the Earth
And brother, hate ain't better
It's just another kind of worse

[Verse 3]
We nice guys love a fallen cause
World peace or Esperanto
At night we march with John Brown
In our dreams and hate Monsanto
But maybe now all this righteous rage
Is just full-speed in reverse
Yeah, brother, it ain't better
It's just another kind of worse

[Verse 4]
"Let's drive racists back underground"
Your bumper sticker said
As if a problem buried deep
Is as good as gone or dead
You promise we'll see paradise
If we kill all the bad guys first
But brother, death ain't better
It's just another kind of worse

[Verse 5]
B7
And I accuse good folks like me

   Em
Of gloating that we're nice

    B7
Then when you crack the surface

```
       Em
You find envy, fear, and vice

    C
We smile as though we like you

       Em
But our virtue's all rehearsed

    Am
We preach on the planet while we plan out

       Em
The beach tours we deserve

         C
Tell me, how are we a step up

       Em
From the sinners that we curse?

   B7
No brother, we ain't better

         C    B7   Em
We're just another kind of worse

       B7
Listen, brother, we ain't better

         C    B7   Em
We're just another kind of worse
```

The Nightingale Won't Let You Sleep

[Capo 5, so actual fingerpicked chords are Dm, C, A, etc., tempo: 138–140 bpm]

[Pulse]
Am Am7 Am Amsus2 Am G G7/F E Fmaj#11/E Am :||

[Theme 1]
Fmaj7 Am D7sus2 F6add#11add14 E Am :||

[Theme 2]
G Gadd2 G Em7#5add12 Csus4 C Em7b13 Em7#5 E
[run down to Am] :|| Am FM#11/E E

[Theme 3]
Eaddb9 E E+7add12 E Eaddb9 E E7 E7b11sus4 E7

E+7add12 E+add12 Am [Return to pulse and repeat whole]

Always Almost Leaving

[Capo 2, so actual chords differ]
[G chord with D: 320033]

[Verse 1]

      C   D   G
We're always almost leaving
              C   D G
But in the end we never part
      C   D   G
We're always almost leaving
         C   D
Then we come back to the start

[Verse 2]
But the start is far behind us
And the end's too hard to face
"It's all over but the grieving"
Or so we said so many days

[Verse 3]
We're almost always leaving
But in the end we never do
I left again this morning
Tonight I'm here with you

[Verse 4]
They say that safe in harbour
Is no place for a ship to be
But it's rougher than an ocean here
And as deep as any sea

[Chorus]

        C   D   Em
There's a shore between sleep and waking

        C   D   G
Between helplessness and power

        C   D   G
There's a line between whole and breaking

        C   D
It can vanish in an hour

[Verse 5]
We're always almost leaving
But in the end we never can
Last night we took two different roads
Yet we wake as one again

[Instrumental, same chord pattern as verses]

[Chorus]
There's a shore between sleep and waking
And between helplessness and power
There's a line between whole and breaking
They'll change places in an hour   [hold D for key shift: D E A]

[Verse 6, same pattern but D E A]

      D   E   A
But the days turn into decades

      D   E   A
And that life was lives ago

      D   E   A
Now we stand on different stages

```
         D        E
And we improvise alone
```

[Verse 7, same as 6]
Some see life as one long goodbye
Some hear only *hello*
Some say all good things must die
Some believe that they just flow

```
         D        E      F#m
They say that safe in harbour
         D        E      A
Is no place for a ship to hide
         D        E      A
To wake is to feel wind fill your sails
         E              A
On a course to lives untried
```

GINGER PHARAND

Wolfe Island gig, September 2, 2021

New Year's Song

[Capo 2]

[G played with D on B string: 320033]
[C played with G on high E string: 032013]

[// = hold chord instead of flowing straight into next line]

[Verse 1]

```
G                    D G      //
Now I understand the altar call
   C            G        //
I've been that close to dying
                   D  G     //
Now I read the rabbi's moving lips
         C              G      //
On the sickbed where he's lying
         D
And the refugee adrift at sea
         C           G
When it seems no god's replying
                   D G       //
Repeat the call, I swear that I'll
         C              G
Come forward, bent and crying
```

56

[Verse 2, same chord pattern, but the "holds" differ]
Now I know the man who turns to pills   //
His life left unattended
The punch-drunk boxer broods alone   //
He once was a contender
And another who loves so deeply
She's completely undefended
Repeat the call, I swear that I'll
Come forward and surrender

[Key shift to A]

[Verse 3]
A   E A
Now I understand the priest who fears
         D   A   //
He's sold his flock a fable
                          E A
The man who bets his hopes and debts
         D   A   //
With no aces for the table
E
The girl who calms her friends with song
             D   A
Though she's scared and barely stable
                      E   A   // ?
Repeat the call, I swear that I'll
         D   A
Come forward if I'm able

[Bridge]

Am   D
I once believed in love received—

      Em   C   [run down to Am]
You're saved by the love they gave you—

Am   D
Now I see it the other way—

        B7   Em   [climb up to G]
Yeah, only love you give can save you

[Key shift again to A]

[Verse 4]

                  E A
Now I understand the gospel choir

      D   A   //
And the Muslim cantor's singing

                E A
The chant of freedom marchers when

      D   A   //
The bells of change are ringing

    E
The sentenced one who greets the sun

        D   A
Though he knows what dawn is bringing

            E A
Repeat the call, I swear that I'll

      D   A   //
Embrace this new beginning

                    A E A
Repeat the call, repeat the call
        D   A
And I'll come forward singing

GINGER PHARAND

Kingston gig, October 5, 2021

NEW
SONGS

Read the Sign

Lyrics by Steven Heighton and Ginger Pharand
Music by Steven Heighton

[Capo 2]

[Spoken]
The trip home's all tail lights
And every time it seems farther
Funny how the radio signal dying out
Makes the road seem so much darker . . .
[Sung]
In the wake of your loving, my will's broken down
I pull off the highway, head back into town

Riff repeats | F#m7/Bm7 |

[Verse 1]

F#m7/Bm7   F#
You're my curse and you're my cure

F#m7/Bm7   F#
You're my doctor and you're my undoer

F#m7/Bm7   F#
You drag me under, then you haul me clear

F#m7/Bm7   F#
You're the puzzle I prayed for, you're the answer I fear

[Bridge 1]

D   A   F#m
Will it be more pain, will it be mercy

      Bm   C#7
All the ways that I hurt you, all the ways that you hurt me
Riff repeats | F#m7/Bm7 |

[Verse 2]
First, you're a fixture, then there's barely a trail
You're fixing to anchor, then you're raising a sail
You're weighing the verdict, but your thumb's on the scale
You hand down the sentence, then you lend me the bail

[Bridge 2]

              D   A
But could it be the light must change

           F#m
Before we'll read the sign

           Dm
You've gotta sacrifice the grape

           C#7
If you want to free the wine

[Instrumental over basic riff—"slide guitar? Maybe blues harp?"]

Riff repeats | F#m7/Bm7 |

[Verse 3]
You say I'm your freedom and your quarantine
I'm the lies that you tell, I'm the truths you mean
But each time you dissolve me, you solve me as well
You burst the bubble, then you cast the spell

[Bridge 3]

       D   A

I used to dream of things that seemed

                F#m

And not the facts that bless me

        Bm

I used to want the world for free

                  C#7

Now I bless the gifts that test me

Riff repeats | F#m7/Bm7 |

In the wake of your loving, my will's broken down
I pull off the highway, head back into town

[Now riff fading out & with slide guitar—late-night car radio fade-out, into static, like a signal dying]

I pull off the highway, head back into town
You're the blues I play, you're the praises I shout
You're the sins I pay for, you're the blessings I count
You're the love that feeds me, you're the test that I need
You're the work that comes easy, you're the words that I bleed . . .

READ THE SIGN

Spoken

The trip home's all taillights
And every time it seems farther
Funny how the radio signal dying out
Makes the road [seem] so much darker . . .

Sung

In the wake of your loving, my will's broken down
I pull off the highway, head back in

You're my curse and you're m
You're my doctor and you're
You drag me under, then y
You're the puzzle I pray

Bridge 1

Will it be more pain,
All the ways that I hu

First you're a fixtu
You're fixing t

2 May 2020
capo 2
bpm 122-124

May 28 j

play
it
120

also
it

G-B-E

1/2/3

GINGER PHARAND

66

Buddha of Song
for John Prine

6/8 Medium tempo

Open G
[Verse 1]

  G   D
I'll tell you a good one if you promise to laugh

      C   D   G
Yeah, punchlines I always get wrong

  G   D
I'm better at writing a sad epitaph

                              G
That's why I envy the Buddha of song

[Verse 2]
I heard he had a mail route and wrote his tunes en route
Humming lines as he ambled along
Wish he'd bring one last letter, help make us feel better
'Cause it's lonelier here on Earth now

[Verse 3]
One way he was magic, he took what was tragic
Made you smile, weep, and still sing along
And I know that you cried on the night that John died
'Cause we'd all lost a Buddha of song

[Chorus]

G   D
John, John you're a Buddha of song

                                                      C   G
And if you'd just write us one more we'd all sing along

       G   D
John, John you're a Buddha of song

D
And if you'd play one more encore we'd all ask for one more

              C   G
And we'll all sing along

[Verse 4]
So now when I reflect on my minor laments
I can't but feel I've gone wrong
If I don't make you smile too, the words are ill-spent
Just listen to the Buddha of song

[Verse 5]
John, be my teacher, I'm a trainable creature
And I'll try not to get it all wrong
Who better for a tutor than a folk music Buddha
A true Bodhisatva of song

[Chorus]

[Verse 6]
Now along the Green River all the willows hang lower
Like somehow they've guessed that he's gone
Up in Paradise with cocktails of vodka and ginger
And cigarettes seven miles long

[Verse 7]
When grieving folks gather, he said that he'd rather
They not bury him cold in the ground
John, please be assured that we heard every word
And we're down here just passing you 'round

[Chorus]

Too Soon to Go

G
I understood how you had to grieve

                         Em
It was what your crushed heart owed

   C   G
But at dark I led you home from the grave

                  D
Though you were loath to go

  G
And as I poured you a second glass

  Em
I said, "Dad, I know that you know

 C   G
There's another dawn beyond this loss

  D   G
But for now, you just can't go"

G
The child was not a woman yet

                 Em
But neither was she a girl

        C   G
And the first time with a broken heart

          D
It feels like a broken world

G
She could not let me dry her tears

                 Em
But I knew as I watched them flow

C   G
There's another dawn beyond this loss

         Em   G
In your own good time you'll be ready to cross

       D   G
But it's still too soon to know

G
Fifty-five's no age to lose

                 Em
Your job and your family

         C   G
But when it comes to the hardest blows

              D
There's no good age to be

G
And I recall my friend saying, "Please

                Em
Tell me what I already know—"

C   G
There's a richer dawn beyond this loss

         Em   G
And my heart some day will be ready to cross

       D   G
But it's still too soon to go

[G| Am] x 4

G
"I never meant to break your heart"

             Em
That's a line that we've all heard

    C   G
But I think now when she said it me

          D
She meant it, every word

 G
Even then I sensed deep down

              Em
What I could not bear to know

C   G
There's some deeper dawn beyond this loss

   Em   G
There'll come a day I'll be ready to cross

     D   G
But for now I just can't go

G
And last I think of the boy we lost

             Em
Before I ever called his name

  C   G
And though some twenty years have passed

         D
I can see him all the same

G
And if I could hold him one more time

      Em
I'd say, "Lie, Son, and tell me it's so—

 C   G
There's another land beyond this loss

 Em   G
And you'll be waiting when I come across

    D   G
Though it's still too soon to go"

The Meteor of the War

Lyrics from "The Portent" by Herman Melville, 1861

[Intro]
Em D C7 Am

[Verse 1]
Riff repeats [Am | Dm/C, Am]
Hanging from the beam,
Swaying in the breeze,
   (that's the law)
Gaunt the shadow on your green,
               Shenandoah!

G7
The cut is on the crown

   Fmaj7/Dm   Am
   (Lo, John Brown),

Am   Dm/C   Am
And the stabs shall heal no more.

            | Fmaj7/Dm, Am | Fmaj7/Dm, Am |
        Shenandoah!   Shenandoah!

[Verse 2]
Hidden in the cap
   Is the anguish none can draw;
So your future veils its face,
   Shenandoah!
But the streaming beard is shown
   (Lo, John Brown),
The meteor of the war.
   Shenandoah! Shenandoah!

Shenandoah! Shenandoah!
Shenandoah! Shenandoah!

Repeat | Fmaj7/Dm, Am | on "Shenandoah!"

[Play through again and finish with "Shenandoah," traditional,
two verses: "I long to see you" and "I'm bound to leave you" fading out
on the last verse]

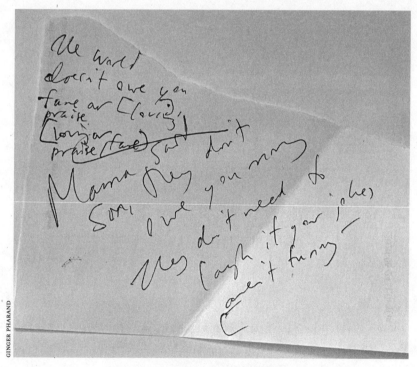

From the file folder "Song Ideas"

The Butcher's Bill

172 bpm

[Capo 5]
Am Dsus2/A Dm9A Em

[Verse 1]
Am7
A boy looks better in a uniform

Am
Sign him up now while they're blowing that horn

 E7   Dm
Don't delay—wars these days

Am7
They never last long

[Verse 2]
Sign 'em up, ship 'em out while the game's on
The kids they'll kill never die with names on
If yours die too, well, they'll do us proud
Patriot angels with a flag as a shroud

[Verse 3]
There's always room in the ranks for fodder
We'll take your son, we'll take your daughter
We'll provide the plane to fly on
We'll supply a hill to die on

[Bridge]

     Dm7
There are bad folks there for our kids to kill

     Am7   E7
And no one ever audits the butcher's bill

     Am7
The butcher's bill

[Verse 4]
The Man likes best when the boys are poor
Or Black, or both at once
It's just a fact, it's just the way it goes
It's how the deck is stacked
(It's the ancient pact.)

[Verse 5]
Each crook-in-chief and high commander
Owes his ranks to propaganda
It's all the same, it's a shame it's a sham
It's a shell game, from Iran to Flanders

[Verse 6]
Sign 'em up now while the signing's good
They'll stand in a row—any citizen should
There's always another few bootcamps full
In America the dutiful
(Russia, China, Canada too.)

[Bridge 2]
There are Brown folks there for our kids to kill
And no one ever audits the butcher's bill
The butcher's bill
(Yeah, the butcher still.)

[Verse 7]

I remember how back in '91
You puppets promised, "We can get this won
In no time," and then you said, "Game on"
And "Job done"... Guess you were lying

[Verse 8]

And then all the talk was about Iraq
How we're going back, and Afghanistan
And it's all the same, it's a sham it's a shame
It's a shell game—it's all Vietnam
(God damn.)

[Verse 9]

I found one son out among the slain
I found the other and he called my name
Said, "A brother looks better in a uniform
But the soul inside it, once torn is torn"

[Bridge 3]

Asleep like sheep on a heroes' hill
And no one ever settles the butcher's bill
The butcher's bill
Yeah, the butcher's will

[Verse 10]

("Mrs. McGrath," the sergeant said,
"Would you like a soldier of your son Ted?
A scarlet coat and big cocked hat
Now Mrs. McGrath would you like that?"
With a too-rye-too-rye-too-rye-ay ...) [repeat to fade]

Still Ain't Misbehavin'

With a tip of the straw hat to Leon Redbone

2/4 Rag 116 bpm

[Capo 5]

G   D7   Em   B7   C   G   A7   Am   D7   D

[Verse 1]

G   D7
Girl, I'm saving all my misbehaving

Em   B7   C
You're the only one worth caving into—

G (stop)
Now I begin to

Am   Am7 D7   D7/F#
See how laying low can be a win too

[Verse 2]

G   D7
When you're gone, girl, I'm all but dormant

Em   B7
It ain't no hardship, no, it ain't no torment

C   G (stop)
Saving the bubbly to toast us doubly

Am   A7   D7   D7/F#
I'm not for sale and for sure I ain't for rent

| G | Am, D7 |

[Verse 3]

G   D7
I used to be one for misdemeanours

Em   B7
Now I'm home eating beans and wieners

C   G stop
Clearing my inbox, washing my sweat socks

Am   A7   D7   D7/F# (stop)
All my old friends say that I'm just a keener
(for you)

[Verse 4]
Girl, I'm saving all of my raving
All my clubbing and my late-night craving
Stay put and pay bills, sweat on the treadmill
These nights it feels right to sit tight waiting
(for you)

[Verse 5]
When it comes to ill intentions
I got none here I'd have to mention
Until you return, I trim my sideburns
Build us a deck and maybe even an extension

[Instrumental: mouth trumpet, trombone, guitar, ragtime piano]

[Key change up to Ab]

| Am | Bb, Eb7 |

[Verse 6]

Ab   Eb
When you're not here, there's no transgressing

 Fm   C7
(It's more as if I'm convalescing)

 Db   Ab (stop)
This social distance needs no assistance

Bbm ·Bb7 Eb7   Eb7/G
And not one sin that requires confessing

[Verse 7]

When it comes to misbehaviour
You're my one and only saviour
When you're lacking, I send Satan packing
Hand me the form now and I'll sign the waiver
(for you)

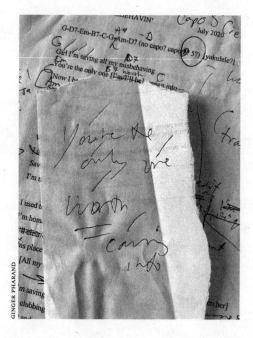

"Roaring drunk"
first draft lines of
"Still Ain't Misbehavin'"

Want It All on Credit

[Capo 2]
Am F F E E Am B7

[Verse 1]

Em
You dream of being Dalai Lama–wise
        C   B7   Em
But without all the trials, admit it
Em
You want to see through an Einstein's eyes
        C   B7   Em
But science? You never read it

      Am
And as for the road that climbs that crest

Em   B7
You never cared to tread it

Em
Some want to get there without ever going
          C   B7   Em
And to pay for the trip on credit

[Verse 2]
Said I was brave as Bolívar
But when trouble came, I fled it
I yearned to earn me a purple heart
But blood? I never bled it
I coveted medals to flash and fill in
The hole my soul inhabited

I needed salutes, I needed attributes
And I craved them all on credit

[Verse 3]
Love—we swear that it must live free
But somehow we never let it
We sing, "Let it flow, let it ride, let it be"
But in the end we'll always try to net it
We talk of a life without hooks or chains
But we don't seem to have led it
In the end we guess we really can own it all
Yeah, possess it all on credit

[Verse 4]
Some say they want to write like the Bard
But they can't be arsed to edit
They say it's gospel passion in their heart
But their spirit, they never fed it
They mean to paint their masterpiece
But not if they'll have to sweat it
Some want to order their fame online
And to claim it today on credit

[Bridge: half-time beat, maybe 66 bpm, mournful Russian interlude,
then return to full-time]

Am Dm Am E C G Dm E
Am G C Dm Am Dm E, then back into the opening riff

[Verse 5]
If there's a pledge or promise that you could keep
I don't suppose you've pled it
If there's a principle you hold dear
I don't believe you've ever met it

Love can't breathe in your bunker of gold—
You don't know enough to regret it
You think it's a fact if you're in the black
That you'll earn some eternal credit

[Verse 6]
You still can't see how your life is graced
You just take all the good for granted
Not one small gift falls to your embrace
But you dream up some way to dread it
I glimpse that full house in your hand
Have you got the balls to bet it?
In the end you lose what you choose not to choose
Life gave it to you all on credit

Looking Back

Bb

[Verse 1]

            Eb   Bb
Together we spent our time
            F   Gm
It left us both broke and tired
            Eb   Bb
Like two words I could not rhyme
            F   Bb
Much as the scheme required
              Eb   Bb
We covered those torch songs fine
            F   Gm
Until we both ran out of fire
              Eb   Bb
Like a ballad that lacks one line
            F   Bb
A chorus in search of a choir

[Verse 2]
You say you collect our love
In letters I sent before
It's all there in black and white
Preserved in a bedroom drawer
But woman go look again
There's nothing that does not age

Our words will read different now
This face is a line-filled page

[Bridge]

Cm   Ab maj   Eb
And if you look for me, you will find I'm gone

       Bb   F   Ab
Like a night the dawn burned away

[Verse 3]
When I look back from here
I feel that I see things true
Each word and detail seems clear
I'm sure it's the same for you
But knowing all life's revised
Is more than a heart can bear
To know we're all improvised
To know what we see wasn't there

[Bridge]

Cm   Ab maj   Eb
And if I look for you, now I find you're gone

       Dadd9/F#   A C
Like a tide from shore pulled away

[Instrumental bridge, then |Abm| and back into main theme]

[Verse 4]
As I look back tonight
I know I can't grasp the whys
The when and the where seem right
But how does a strong thing die?

I guess nothing green abides
And rust overruns desire
Some say the world ends in ice
But I think it ends with fire

[Bridge]
Still, if you look for us you will find we're gone
Even clouds that merge burn away

Orpheus

[Start in G, G1, or G2 / key shift to A with heavy backbeat]

[Verse 1]

G
I'll hold my breath the whole way down

    C
And find your soul in the undertown

   G
An Orpheus, he never feels a chill

     C
He's got a killer's nerve and a lover's will

    D
As a willow sings when the wind whips through

   Em   C
His lungs are filled with hymns for you

   G
His guitar ringing like a minstrel's lyre

   C   G
He'll sing for your ransom and he'll never tire

[Verse 2]
As a holy man never dreads the tomb
As a con man knows he can charm the room
Orpheus, he put his faith in song
His fingers flying as he sang along
And serenading like a one-man choir
Said, "My woman loves me like a four-bell fire
I won't be leaving till I see her face

88

Take her hand and lead her free of this place."

[Key shift to A]

[Verse 3]

A

Hades said, "Son, you can keep your tunes

    D

We're not short of crooners here in the tombs."

    A

But love and grief will lift a man's voice higher

      D

And he laid it down just like a one-man choir

      E

Well, Hades wiped away his tears and said

      Bm   D

Like the devil in Georgia when he bowed his head,

    A

"You win, this once I'll let you lead her free

      D   A

But don't look till you're there or she returns to me."

[Verse 4]
Well, if you make a deal with the mafia
Don't try to take more than they offer ya
She said, "I know your eyes are for me alone
But keep them on the road, honey, till we're home."
The legend says the lover got it wrong
But, hell, that's a myth and this is my damn song
I say the singer kept his word and his wife
And by dawn they had made it to a second life

[Verse 5]

Now Orpheus, he covers sweeter tunes
In the smaller clubs, and he still charms rooms
But his voice don't soar like it used to sound
Now it rumbles low like it grew from the ground
Some say what wore it down was time
Or late-night talks, cigarettes, and wine
But I think he's dialled into a frequency
To tell Mr. Hell, "We're up here and we're free."

From footage for the Eden Mills Writers' Festival, 2021

(Still Mean to) Make Your Way Across

[Capo 2]

CsusF   Am7   Em7

[Verse 1]

A   F#m
We make you learn it all alone

        A   F#m
Until the solitude's the only thing you own

        A   F#m
Don't let your fears show if you want to seem full-grown

        G   A   F#m
Your body's almost there but your soul's just skin and bone

[Chorus]

D   F#m
Still mean to make your way across

D   F#m
But the canyon nights are cold and without a guide you're lost

D   A
We should have shown you how to make the stars your chart

G   F#m
No need to kill or score or die to make your mark

[Verse 2]
We teach you how to add, not how to know what counts
How to weigh your worth in profit, praise, or pounds
Don't let your conscience show if you want to seem to count
You scan these rooms for men and all you see are clowns

[Instrumental trumpet]

[Verse 3]
We key you up with screens, we calm you down with meds
Deep-fake naked dreams in imaginary beds
Pushers in the penthouse sell you your dopamine instead
Or tell you seek your dreams and sell you scams instead

[Chorus]
Still mean to make your way across
But the winter nights get cold and without a guide you're lost
We gave you no clear path, no path that you could trust
So you've no compass now but you're thinking someone must

Jacob's Angel

Lyrics by Steven Heighton and Ginger Pharand
Music by Steven Heighton

[Duet in double drop-D tuning]

[He:]

Em
I set out for Morgantown
With murder on my mind
I was loath to leave my family
But a killer was mine to find

Cmaj7
All night we'd kept our grieving
The ground too cold to break

Em
By a candlelit pine casket
Where our only boy lay slain

[She:]
My love left armed for Morgantown
To answer for our son
But in his haste and sorrowing
He left behind one gun

I took up my man's rifle
From underneath our bed
And followed to watch over him
And help justify the dead

[He:]
I'd aimed to seek out Jacob Crow
In the taverns of the town
But he drew a bead from where the woods stay green
And the coward gunned me down

I felt my life bleed fast away
To the pounding of my pulse
But the sound was only hoofbeats
Approaching from the south

[Bridge]
[He:]

Cmaj7
Is this shadow that steals over me

B7
The dark, cold wing of Death?

[She:]

Em
No, my love, I've come to you
See your blood stains my dress

[Chorus—in harmony]

    G
In the Good Book, Jacob's angel came

  Em
To bless him and to save

  Cmaj7
But this one comes with loaded gun

Em
To lay you in the grave

[He:]
Oh no, my love, turn back for home
Let heaven settle scores
But she whispered this vow in my ear,
"He won't have to wait on the Lord"

[She:]
Hang, I won't, hang on, you will
My love, you will survive
The only men I've ever loved
Will not lay side by side

[Chorus—in harmony]
In the Good Book, Jacob's angel came
To bless him and to save
But this one comes with loaded gun
To lay you in the grave

The Last Living Woman Alive

[Am, capo 3, 4, or 5]

[Intro and instrumental bridge]
Am7   Dm7 [xx0221]   Cmaj7   Fmaj7/A   Bm7b5 [x20201]
Esus4   E7   [pause]
Am7   Dm7   G   Cmaj7   Fmaj7/A   Bm7b5   Esus4   E   Am

[Verse 1]
Am
You hear her talking and she's dropping no names

                                    Am7   Dm [run
down, D, Db, C, B]
There's no one she's knocking, no, she's not one for playing those games

     Am
Like all the ones you thought would help you survive

      E   Bm7b5   Esus4   E   Am
Now it feels like you're talking to the last living woman alive

[Verse 2]
You see her working 'cause it's got to get done
She won't be shirking, she don't think she's the only one
Who's got to shift a lot of shit to get by
Now it feels like you're working with the last living woman alive

[Bridge]

    Dm

Your mother might say, "Son, what were you thinking

    Am

A woman that strong'll just drive you to drinking"

    Dm **[bossa nova run down again]**

Well, if this is strong liquor, you can fill up my pitcher

    Bm7b5   Esus4 E

With a shot for the devil and a pint for the preacher

[Instrumental bridge—half-time bossa nova]

[Verse 3]

You catch her crying and you want to ask why

She's not one for lying—you might not want to hear her reply

It's here that fear and loving collide

When it feels like you're failing the last living woman alive

[Verse 4]

You watch her dreaming as the moon comes up

You pray God keeps her, that the love that you give her's enough

For all the blues she helped you sing through the nights

And now it seems like you're singing for the last living woman alive

[Bridge]

Papa might say, "You didn't think this through

A woman this smart'll make a fool out of you"

Well, if this is my lesson, I'm finished with guessing

I'm tired of cheating and I'm ready for testing

[Instrumental bridge]

[Vocal bridge]

C#m   A   E

Your pride made you boast you could do it alone

C#m   D   A

Push that weight up the slope, whether spirit or stone

F#   C#m   B

Day in, day out, till you're withered to bone

[Verse 5]

When the day's a desert and your roots need rain
Your fears are fetters and you feel you're all alone in your chains
You know there's someone in the dark on your side
Now it feels like you're leaning on the last living woman alive

Kitchen composing, January 2022

CODA

Grief is most frequently described as occurring in waves and, were that true here, it would be a natural parallel, linking to sound waves and musical movements. The reality of bringing this book to press, however, in the year and a half following Steve's death, was a far less elegant arc. Grief, as the bereaved learn quickly and well, pierces you at its own rhythm, on its count, not in cycles but with sniper fire, a live wire shock, a crowbar behind the knees, a snare under leaves. The truth of it is less orchestral and more gut-bucket blues. In his work, Steve was meticulous in capturing the raw footage of life, the peculiar intimacies of living in this fragile mortal form and how those moments weave into the field of a larger human experience. This book of his music was, fittingly, a microcosm of that same churning of stark and sublime energies. And because I could not have stumbled through it without the care and support of others, I want to use this space to say thank you to a few otherwise hidden hands that helped this project into the world.

A book of cowboy chords and lyrics was I'm sure not the obvious choice for ECW Press and yet Michael Holmes has been a careful and constant shepherd of this work from the start. When Steve first asked me to do the book in March 2022, he assured me, "Just talk to Michael. He won't let us down." And he was right. Not for a second did I ever feel I couldn't go to Michael. His unwavering support is the chief reason this book exists.

Likewise, "the golden ears" of Chris Brown of Wolfe Island Records were crucial to verifying my manuscript and helping me translate scribbles, video clips, and my voice into chords (and ultimately the score) for the unpublished songs. As the producer of *The Devil's Share*, Chris brought his deep knowledge of Steve's songwriting and playing and vision for his music into our sessions. For over a year, I was the only living person who knew and could sing the melody line for all of the unrecorded songs to accompany Steve's chords. That Chris Brown was the first to hear them in their entirety was natural and deeply healing.

To those who helped with suggestions, stories, and permissions, much gratitude. Specifically, John Heighton, Mary Huggard, Kevin Bowers, and Angie Abdou. And a stand-alone thank you to Una McDonnell. Una stepped in with support in whatever way it was needed and there were a few days when she was the sole source of progress.

At ECW Press, the production team were helpful, patient, and thorough. Special thanks to Production Co-ordinator Victoria Cozza and Jen Albert, who returned a clean copyedit for a beast of a project. Jessica Albert gave personal attention and exceptional care to her cover design.

"The Meteor of the War" was taken from Herman Melville's "The Portent" and developed from a conversation with Julian Scala. The song is dedicated to him.

Because the new songs have never been heard, and it is impossible to know a melody from the chords alone, please look out for the lead sheets and score that are available for download from Wolfe Island Records. There will also be Wolfe Island "porch session" recordings available online soon to bring the tunes to life for those who want to play them. For access to the songs from the first album, *The Devil's Share* is available online at the WIR website: https://wolfeislandrecords.com/stevenheighton/.

GINGER PHARAND

Steven Heighton (1961–2022) was a musician and the award-winning author of twenty books of poetry, nonfiction, and fiction, including the *New York Times Book Review* Editor's Choice *Afterlands* and *The Waking Comes Late*, winner of the Governor General's Award for Poetry. In 2021, he released his first album, *The Devil's Share*. He lived in Kingston, Ontario.

Ginger Pharand is a literary editor, educator, and psychotherapist. Originally from South Carolina, she lives in Kingston, Ontario.

This book is also available as a Global Certified Accessible™ (GCA) ebook. ECW Press's ebooks are screen reader friendly and are built to meet the needs of those who are unable to read standard print due to blindness, low vision, dyslexia, or a physical disability.

At ECW Press, we want you to enjoy our books in whatever format you like. If you've bought a print copy or an audiobook not purchased with a subscription credit, just send an email to ebook@ecwpress.com and include:

- the book title
- the name of the store where you purchased it
- a screenshot or picture of your order/receipt number and your name

A real person will respond to your email with your ePub attached. If you prefer to receive the ebook in PDF format, please let us know in your email.

Some restrictions apply. This offer is only valid for books already available in the ePub format. Some ECW Press books do not have an ePub format for us to send you. In those cases, we will let you know if a PDF format is available as an alternative. This offer is only valid for books purchased for personal use. At this time, this program is not offered on school or library copies.

Thank you for supporting an independently owned Canadian publisher with your purchase!